"You're gonna regret this."

"We are?" said Mr. Pepperday.

"Yeah," said Tooter. "You can drag me out of here, but there's one thing you can't make me do."

For the last time, the Pepperday family left their house in Morgantown.

"You're not giving me the silent treatment, are you?" said Mr. Pepperday.

There was no answer. Tooter's lips were clamped tight.

First Stepping Stone Books you will enjoy:

By David A. Adler
(The Houdini Club Magic Mystery series)
Onion Sundaes
Wacky Jacks

By Kathleen Leverich
Brigid Bewitched
Brigid Beware!

By Mary Pope Osborne
(The Magic Tree House series)
Pirates Past Noon (#4)
Night of the Ninjas (#5)

By Barbara Park
Junie B. Jones and Her Big Fat Mouth
Junie B. Jones and Some Sneaky Peeky Spying

By Louis Sachar
Marvin Redpost: Why Pick on Me?
Marvin Redpost: Alone in His Teacher's House

By Marjorie Weinman Sharmat
(The Genghis Khan Dog Star series)
The Great Genghis Khan Look-Alike Contest
Dog-Gone Hollywood

By Jerry Spinelli
Tooter Pepperday

By Camille Yarbrough
Tamika and the Wisdom Rings

Tooter Pepperday

by Jerry Spinelli

illustrated by
Donna Nelson

A FIRST STEPPING STONE BOOK
Random House New York

For Jim Trelease

*I am grateful to the Katkowski family—Moses, Fred, and Jean—
and to Leslie Jones for their assistance; and to Shauna Pepperday
for lending me her name.*   —*J. S.*

Text copyright © 1995 by Jerry Spinelli.
Illustrations copyright © 1995 by Donna Nelson.
All rights reserved under International and Pan-American Copyright
Conventions. Published in the United States by Random House, Inc.,
New York, and simultaneously in Canada by Random House of Canada
Limited, Toronto.

Library of Congress Cataloging-in-Publication Data
Spinelli, Jerry. Tooter Pepperday / by Jerry Spinelli.
   p. cm. "A First stepping stone book." SUMMARY: Hating to leave
her familiar surroundings, Tooter resorts to sabotage when her family
moves from their suburban home to Aunt Sally's farm.
ISBN 0-679-84702-2 (trade) — ISBN 0-679-94702-7 (lib. bdg.)
[1. Moving, Household—Fiction. 2. Behavior—Fiction.
3. Farm life—Fiction. 4. Humorous stories.] I. Title.
PZ7.S75663To 1995 [Fic]—dc20 94-25689

Manufactured in the United States of America   10 9 8 7 6 5 4 3 2

Random House, Inc. New York, Toronto, London, Sydney, Auckland

Contents

1

Never!

"Tooter," said Mr. Pepperday. "I'll ask you one more time. Where is the key?"

When Mr. Pepperday was mad, his nose got red. His nose was now as red as a strawberry.

Tooter Pepperday snarled. "I'll never tell. Not even if you torture me."

They were in the bathroom.

Mr. Pepperday stepped back to the doorway. "The truck is loaded. Your mother and brother are waiting. We are leaving. Are you coming with us?"

"Never!"

Mr. Pepperday turned and went down the stairs. His footsteps echoed off the bare walls and floors. The house was empty.

The U-Haul truck was at the curb.

Mrs. Pepperday looked down from the driver's seat. "Where's Tooter?"

"She's not coming," said Mr. Pepperday. "She doesn't want to go."

Mrs. Pepperday groaned. "We already know that. The whole world knows. Why didn't you just drag her out here?"

"I can't."

"You can't?"

"No. She's handcuffed herself to the pipe under the bathroom sink."

Mrs. Pepperday rolled her eyes to the sky. "Help me."

Chuckie Pepperday was Tooter's little brother.

"Go, Tooter!" he yipped.

He jumped from the truck and ran into the house for a look.

"Don't handcuffs have a key?" said Mrs. Pepperday. "Where's the key?"

"She won't tell. Not even under torture, she said."

Mrs. Pepperday looked up at the bare windows of the red brick house.

"Torture, huh?" She nodded. "We'll see."

Mr. and Mrs. Pepperday went into the house and up to the bathroom. They found Chuckie standing in the doorway. He was stone still, staring. Tooter was sitting on the floor under the sink. She was hugging the water pipe. Her right wrist was joined to the pipe with Chuckie's toy handcuffs.

"Pull her away from the pipe," said Mrs. Pepperday to her husband. "I want the armpit."

Chuckie saw what was coming. He shuddered. "Uh-oh."

Tooter's eyes bulged in terror. "Oh no!" She squeezed the water pipe. "Oh no you don't!"

Mrs. Pepperday's voice was calm. "Are you going to tell me where the key is?"

"Never."

"Peel her off."

Mr. Pepperday peeled Tooter away until her only attachment to the pipe was the handcuffs.

"Pull the arm out straight."

He pulled the arm out straight.

Chuckie fled from the bathroom. "I don't wanna see!"

Mrs. Pepperday knelt down.

Tooter screamed, "No! Don't!"

But her mother was out of mercy. She zeroed in on Tooter's armpit and tickled—

"No! Stop! Ha!"

And tickled—

"Help! Police haha!"

And tickled—until Tooter could only howl with laughter.

At last she gasped, "Shoe! Shoe!"

Mrs. Pepperday stopped tickling.

Mr. Pepperday pulled off Tooter's sneakers. A thin tin key clinked to the floor.

"Yahoo!" Chuckie ran back in. He unlocked the cuffs.

Tooter was free.

Mr. and Mrs. Pepperday each took a hand and walked Tooter downstairs.

Tooter growled, "You're gonna regret this."

"We are?" said Mr. Pepperday.

"Yeah," said Tooter. "You can drag me out of here, but there's one thing you can't make me do."

For the last time, the Pepperday family left their house in Morgantown.

"You're not giving me the silent treatment, are you?" said Mr. Pepperday.

There was no answer. Tooter's lips were clamped tight.

2

The Silent Treatment

"Bye, old house."

Chuckie waved as they drove off. He rode in the truck with his mother.

Tooter and her father followed in the car. Tooter did not wave. She did not even look. She grumped in the backseat.

The Pepperdays were moving to Aunt Sally's farm, two states and three hundred miles away. They were moving because they could live for free at Aunt Sally's.

Living for free was a good idea, because the Pepperdays did not have much money.

Mr. Pepperday had quit his job, and Mrs. Pepperday did not earn much driving a school bus.

Aunt Sally had said they would all be "happy as hogs in slop."

Mr. Pepperday was happy. Now he could spend all his time writing books for children.

Mrs. Pepperday was happy. Now she could live on a farm.

Aunt Sally was happy. Now she would have help with the chores. And she could give more time to her beekeeping.

And Chuckie was happy. Now he would get to sleep with Harvey. Harvey was Aunt Sally's rusty, shaggy dog.

"I'm a hog in slop!" Chuckie kept laughing.

Everybody was happy but Tooter. Tooter had a perfectly good life in Morgantown. McDonald's. The tire tunnel at the playground. Saturday morning yard sales. T-ball. Her friends. Especially Matthew Kain, her sidewalk skating buddy.

Tooter had no desire to move to a stupid farm. Farms didn't even have sidewalks. And what did she want with hogs in slop?

She did not speak as her father drove past her favorite snack shop:

PETE'S DELI, HOME OF THE WORLD'S
BEST BARREL PICKLES

She did not speak as he drove past the sign that said:

YOU ARE NOW LEAVING MORGANTOWN.
COME BACK SOON!

She did not speak when they stopped for lunch.

She did not speak during the long drive that afternoon. Or when they arrived at Aunt

Sally's. Or while they unloaded all their things into the farmhouse.

Or during dinner.

Aunt Sally was coating a biscuit with honey when she looked at Tooter and said, "Are you sick?"

"Not sick," said Mrs. Pepperday. "Just not talking."

"The silent treatment," said Mr. Pepperday.

"He hates the silent treatment," said Mrs. Pepperday.

"I hate the silent treatment," said Mr. Pepperday.

"Well now," said Aunt Sally with a sly grin. "Maybe I kinda like it. Maybe we'll have some peace and quiet around here."

"Tooter didn't want to move," said Chuckie. "She hates the farm."

Tooter glared at her brother.

Chuckie rolled on: "Tooter says farms are smelly and ugly and stupid. Tooter says farm

kids are always stepping in cow poop. She says the pigs eat your fingers off while you're sleeping. And the big reason she hates the farm is because Matthew Kain isn't here. She loves him. She wrote him a love letter and she hid it in her suitcase and she's gonna send it to him."

Tooter yelled, "I am not! I do not! I did not!"

She threw a biscuit. It bounced off Chuckie's forehead.

"He lies, the little brat! All I ever did was go roller-skating with Matthew Kain!"

She stopped. Everyone was grinning at her. She mashed her hand to her mouth. But it was too late.

Mr. Pepperday raised his fist in victory. "She talks!"

3

Kicked Out

Next day, after breakfast, Tooter found her father at his computer.

She stood beside him. He kept pecking at the keyboard. With each peck, a new letter appeared on the screen.

She coughed to get his attention. He kept pecking. When Mr. Pepperday was writing, he forgot the rest of the world.

"New book?" said Tooter.

No answer.

"Am I in it?" Tooter always asked him

that. He had not yet put her into one of his books.

No answer.

She sat on the computer table.

He did not notice.

She sat on the keyboard.

He noticed.

The screen went crazy. Mr. Pepperday went crazy. His nose glowed red like a Christmas-tree bulb.

He bellowed: "TOOTERRRRRR! Scoot!"

Tooter scooted.

She decided to check on her mother. She found her downstairs, unpacking glasses.

"What did you do to your father?"

"I sat on his keyboard."

Mrs. Pepperday groaned. "And why did you do that?"

Tooter shrugged. "I don't know. Maybe it's the farm. Ever since I got here I've been feeling goofy."

Tooter's right hand rose slowly until it was beside her head. A finger pointed, then stuck itself into her ear.

"See?" she wailed. "See?" She removed the finger with her left hand. "Who knows what I might do next? We better move back before I do something *really* weird."

"You better stop this silliness," said Mrs. Pepperday. "Before *I* do something."

Tooter's left hand made a fist, swung upward and bopped herself on the head.

"Tooter—out."

Tooter frowned. "You're kicking me out? I'm getting a strange farm disease. I need help." Two fingers crawled up her nose.

"In five more seconds, young lady, you're going to get what you need, and it won't be help. Now, go explore the farm."

"I don't want to explore the farm."

Mrs. Pepperday pointed to the door. "Go."

Tooter went, mumbling. "Kicking me out of the house. My own mother."

Outside, Chuckie came running with Harvey. "Tooter! Come on! Come see all the bees!"

"I don't want to see bees," said Tooter.

"Aunt Sally will give us honey. You love honey. Look!"

He held up a finger gleaming with golden honey. He licked some of it away. Harvey licked off the rest.

Chuckie pulled at Tooter. "Come *on.*"

Tooter would not budge. "I don't love honey. I hate honey. I've hated it since the minute I got here. I'm sick of farm food. I want a Big Mac."

"Where are you going to get a Big Mac?"

"McDonald's. Where else?"

Chuckie looked around. The only buildings they could see belonged to Aunt Sally. The house, the barn, the chicken coop, the honey house. Beyond that all they could see were fields and trees and bright blue sky.

"Where's McDonald's?" said Chuckie.

"There's always a McDonald's around," said Tooter.

She was desperate for a taste of the old neighborhood.

"All you have to do is walk down a road." She started walking. "You coming?"

Chuckie yipped, "Sure!"

Harvey yipped, "Arf!"

Off they went down the road.

4

Do I Believe This?

Mrs. Pepperday stepped out to call everyone in to lunch. A pickup truck pulled up to the front door. In the back were six bales of hay, three young pigs, and two young Pepperdays.

Chuckie jumped out squealing. "I want a pig!"

Tooter got out holding her nose.

The man at the wheel wore a straw hat and a friendly smile. He opened the door. Harvey popped out.

"These yours?" he said to Mrs. Pepperday.

"They're mine," she said.

"Sally told us she had a family moving in," he said. "I'm Burt Tolen, your neighbor. A mile down the road."

"Greta Pepperday."

They shook hands.

"Well," he said, "I'm due home for lunch. I'll let them tell you about it."

Mr. Tolen drove off.

Chuckie blabbered, "Mom, we walked for a hundred miles and we didn't come to a single McDonald's! Not one! Then Mr. Tolen picked us up. Just when my feet were gonna fall off."

Mrs. Pepperday glared at Tooter.

Suddenly Aunt Sally's voice rang out: "You dumb chicken! I know *rocks* that are smarter than you! If I ever catch you, I'll—"

Mrs. Pepperday and the kids dashed across the barnyard.

A brown chicken came flying from the coop.

Aunt Sally followed, shaking her fist. "You're drumsticks! You hear? Drumsticks!"

"What's the trouble?" said Mrs. Pepperday.

"Trouble?" snapped Aunt Sally. She led them inside the coop. She pointed. *"There's* the trouble."

On the dirt floor of the chicken coop were four hen's eggs—smashed.

"I'm trying to raise a handful of chicks," said Aunt Sally. "That mess of feathers out there is supposed to be a brood hen. But every once in a while you get a looney-tune."

She pointed to a shelf near the ceiling. "That dumb drumstick knocked her own eggs off the roost."

She climbed a ladder for a look into the nest of straw. "Well, well. Guess I got here just in time." She held up a brown-shelled egg. "One left."

Cupping it in both hands, Aunt Sally carried the egg into the kitchen.

"You going to scramble it?" said Tooter.

Aunt Sally laughed. "No, I'm going to incubate it. You want to hold it for a minute?"

Tooter drew back. "Not me."

"I'll hold it," piped Chuckie.

Aunt Sally gave the egg to Chuckie. She showed him how to keep it covered with both hands.

"We have to keep it very warm," she explained.

Aunt Sally set to work. She fetched a shoebox and stuffed it with an old pillowcase. She set the shoebox on the floor in a corner of the kitchen. Then she rigged up a bare light bulb so that it hung over the box. She turned on the bulb.

"Okay," she said to Chuckie. "Lay 'er in there. Careful, now."

Carefully, Chuckie laid the egg on the pillowcase.

"This is how we incubate an egg when the mother is a looney-tune," said Aunt Sally. "If all goes well, in about twenty days we'll have ourselves a chick."

"Can I have it for a pet?" said Chuckie.

"We'll see," said Aunt Sally. "But first I need a baby-sitter. Once a day somebody has to give the egg a quarter-turn. So it stays warm all over."

"Me! Me!" yipped Chuckie.

But Aunt Sally was looking elsewhere. "The boy already did one chore. I think this one belongs to his sister."

"I don't," said Tooter.

"I do," said her mother.

"Good," said Aunt Sally. "You're hired."

"What if I don't do it?" said Tooter.

Aunt Sally looked straight at her. "Then the egg will never become a chick."

Tooter slumped away grumbling. "Do I believe this? I was kidnapped away from my happy home in Morgantown. I was smuggled all the way out here. Why? To baby-sit an egg. That's why."

5

You're Nothing Without Me

Next day Mr. Pepperday sat down to his computer. He punched up the chapter book he was working on. Here is what appeared on the screen:

Tooter Pepperday was a wonderful girl. She was kind and friendly and nice to everybody. She lived in Morgantown. She loved her home. She loved to play with her friends.

And then her mean and cruel

```
parents took her away to a
smelly old farm and there was no
McDonald's and Tooter had to
baby-sit an egg.
```

Mr. Pepperday made a printout. He took
it to his wife. She was sanding a bookcase in
the dining room.

"Now Tooter has invaded my computer,"
he told her. "Look at this." He showed her
the printout. "She says we're mean and
cruel."

Mrs. Pepperday chuckled. "All kids say
that. It makes them feel better."

"I don't think she's feeling better at all,"
he said. "I haven't seen her smile since we
left Morgantown. I'm starting to feel guilty
about moving."

"Don't feel guilty," said Mrs. Pepperday.
"That's just what she wants you to do. You
know Tooter. She's a scrapper, that's all.

She can't give up without a fight."

Mr. Pepperday looked around. "Where is she now?"

"Ordering pizza."

"Pizza! In the morning?"

"She says it's been three days now. It's the longest she's ever had to go without pizza. She couldn't wait another minute."

Tooter stomped into the room. She slammed the phone book to the floor. "I don't believe this."

"Believe what?" said Mr. Pepperday.

"Pizza places don't deliver out here. They say it's too far. We're in the middle of nowhere!" She was pacing back and forth, waving her arms, ranting. "If I don't get some pizza pretty quick, I'm not gonna make it. I'm gonna croak!"

Mr. Pepperday took Tooter by both shoulders and sat her down. He studied her face.

He examined her fingernails. He poked through her hair.

"What?" said Tooter.

Mr. Pepperday turned to his wife. He shook his head sadly. "She's right. She's in the final stages of pizza-pie shortage. She may not last the day."

Tooter pushed him away and got up. "Funny, Dad."

Mrs. Pepperday had a good laugh.

She said, "Did you do your chore, Toot?"

"What chore?" said Tooter.

"The egg."

Tooter snorted. "That's so dumb. Who cares if the stupid egg gets turned every day? Would the chicken turn it every day?" She glared at her parents. "Huh?"

No answer.

Tooter decided to show them how silly the whole thing was. She squatted down on the rug as if she were a hen.

She cackled: "Ba-*bawlk* ba-*bawlk*."

She raised up. She peeked under herself.

"Ba-*bawlk*. Oh my goodness, I do believe it's time to turn my egg. Ba-*bawlk*. If I don't

turn it every day, it won't get done on all sides. Ba-*bawlk*. And then when little junior comes out, his hiney will be fuzzy and his head will still be an egg yolk. Ba-*bawlk*."

Mr. and Mrs. Pepperday roared with laughter. And they weren't the only ones.

Mr. Pepperday pointed at Tooter. "She's laughing!"

Tooter stopped laughing at once.

Mrs. Pepperday clapped. "Terrific performance." She gave Tooter a hug. "Now, go do your chore."

Tooter headed for the kitchen.

On the floor, in the corner, in the shoebox, on the pillowcase—the egg was basking inches below the light bulb, its own private little sun.

"This is dumb," Tooter whispered as she gave the egg a quarter-turn. The light brown shell felt warm and perfectly smooth.

Tooter stared at the egg. The more she stared, the more annoyed she became. Who did this egg think it was, anyhow? Just lying there while everybody else had to be its servant.

"Think you're a big deal, don't you?" she said.

The egg did not answer.

"You're nothing without me," Tooter told it. And just to prove it, she put her hand between the light bulb and the egg.

The egg was in shadow. Already Tooter could feel it cooling down. She shaded the egg for five seconds...ten seconds. She thought she might do it for an hour or two. But soon the back of her hand became hot. She took it away.

"That'll teach you who's boss around here," she said. "Don't you ever forget it."

The egg did not answer.

Tooter leaned down until her lips were almost touching the shell.

"Boo," she said.

The egg was silent.

6

Woe Is Me!

"Have you seen Tooter?"

Mrs. Pepperday stood in the office door-way the next morning.

Mr. Pepperday went on writing at his computer.

She said it louder: "Have you seen Tooter?"

Mr. Pepperday kept writing.

Mrs. Pepperday came into the room. She stood behind Mr. Pepperday and rapped the top of his head with her knuckle.

Mr. Pepperday squawked. "Oww!"

"Next time, I sit on your keyboard," said Mrs. Pepperday. "Have you seen Tooter?"

Mr. Pepperday rubbed his head. "No. Why?"

"The morning's half over and I haven't seen her yet. She's not in her room. Do you know where she is?"

"No, but I know where she *was.* Into my computer again." He scrolled up the screen. "This is her latest."

Mrs. Pepperday leaned over his shoulder to read the words on the screen:

```
    Every minute Tooter Pepperday
made a new gruesome discovery
about the farm. Every day she
listened for the bell of the Jack
and Jill ice cream truck but it
never came. There were no movies,
no video arcade, no deli, no
7-Eleven. The TV only had two
```

channels and no cable. And worst
of all nobody would deliver.
Tooter Pepperday was a kid without
pizza.

Tooter Pepperday cried out
loud, "Woe is me!"

"Do you think she took off down the
road again?" said Mr. Pepperday.

"I don't know," said Mrs. Pepperday. "But
I'm going to find out."

She went back downstairs, calling
Tooter's name. She called again and again.
From the front door. From the back door.

Chuckie came running in with Harvey.

"Have you seen your sister?" said Mrs.
Pepperday.

"No," said Chuckie.

"Arf!" said Harvey.

"She's not *your* sister," said Mrs. Pepperday to Harvey.

"Did she run away?" said Chuckie.

Mrs. Pepperday held his chin. "Why do you say that?"

"Because she said she was going to go back home. Even if she had to walk."

Mrs. Pepperday rolled her eyes to the sky. "Help me." She ran to the car.

Chuckie and Harvey hurried after.

"Can we come?" said Chuckie.

"All right, all right. Climb in. Quick."

Chuckie and Harvey jumped into the backseat.

Mrs. Pepperday drove down the road. "Keep a sharp eye out, you two," she said.

"Arf!" said Harvey.

Eight miles she drove. Nine miles. Ten miles.

No Tooter.

She turned around and drove twenty miles the other way.

Still no Tooter.

She drove back to the farmhouse.

"Are we going to call the police, Mom?" said Chuckie.

"First I'm calling Mr. Tolen," she said. "Maybe he knows something."

Chuckie and Harvey raced into the kitchen.

Mrs. Pepperday followed. She telephoned the neighbor, Mr. Tolen. He was out in the fields. But Mrs. Tolen said she had not seen a little girl.

Mrs. Pepperday went up to her husband's office.

"I can't find her anywhere."

This time Mr. Pepperday heard the first time. He turned in his chair. They stared at each other. Afraid to speak. Afraid to even think what might have happened to Tooter.

Suddenly Mrs. Pepperday cocked her

head. "What's that noise?"

"What noise?" said Mr. Pepperday.

"*That.*" She moved to the doorway. "Thumping."

She was heading down the hall, following the sound to Tooter's room.

Most of Harvey was under Tooter's bed.

Only his shaggy, rusty tail stuck out. It was
thumping on the floor like a drummer.

"Harvey!" commanded Mrs. Pepperday.

Harvey backed out and came to Mrs.
Pepperday, wagging his tail.

"Tooter," she said. "I'll count to three. One…two…"

On the count of three, Tooter crawled out from under her bed.

7

Right Where You Want to Be

Fifteen minutes later Tooter was standing at the open doorway of the honey house. It was a shed-like building, smaller than her bedroom.

Aunt Sally was inside, washing out metal pails in a large sink. There were more pails, a tall stack of them. There were also tanks and screens and copper pipes and hoses.

"You're supposed to punish me," said Tooter.

Aunt Sally looked up from her work. "Is

that so? Isn't that your mother's job?"

"She did punish me. Now it's your turn."

Aunt Sally let out a slow whistle. "You must have been mighty bad. What did you do?"

"I hid under my bed all morning."

Aunt Sally nodded. "And worried your mother half to death wondering where you were."

Tooter shrugged. "I guess."

"So, how did she punish you?"

"She lectured me for nineteen hours."

Aunt Sally frowned. "Ouch. I reckon that hurt."

"It was gruesome."

"So what am I supposed to do? Make you listen to me sing?"

She reared back and let out a note that sounded like a cow with a toothache.

Tooter clamped her hands over her ears.

"No! Stop! You're supposed to show me the farm."

Aunt Sally's eyebrows shot up. "That's punishment?"

Tooter slumped against the doorway and slid to a seat on the cement floor. "For me it is, I guess. My mother says the only things I've seen are the house and the chicken coop. She says I should see the whole place."

"What else did she say?"

"She says I should stop complaining."

Aunt Sally placed a pail on top of the stack. "What do you say?"

Tooter did not reply at once. She looked away. "I don't want to hurt anybody's feelings."

Aunt Sally flapped her straw hat at Tooter. "Ah, go ahead. I'm a tough old critter. I don't have feelings."

The conversation was getting uncomfortable. Tooter changed the subject. "Aunt Sally, how come you always say words like that?"

"Like what?"

"Like critter. And reckon and yonder."

Aunt Sally chuckled. "Well, it's like this. When I bought this place, I told myself, Sal, ol' gal, you're a farmer now, so act like one. So I bought me a straw hat and started saying words I heard farmers say in the movies. I don't reckon it made me a farmer, but it made me feel like one."

Tooter said, "What does *a hog in slop* mean?"

"If you're a hog in slop," said Aunt Sally, "you're right smack-dab where you want to be."

"My dad says it."

Aunt Sally nodded. "I know. He got it from me. I've been saying it for years."

"I heard my mom and Chuckie say it too."

Aunt Sally gave her a sideways look. "Sounds like everybody around here is a hog in slop but you."

Tooter did not say anything. But she thought, I'll never be a hog in slop. I'll never be right smack-dab where I want to be.

Aunt Sally clapped her hands. "Okay, enough of this mush. Let's get on with the punishment."

8

Punishment

"First of all," said Aunt Sally, "nobody takes a punishment of mine sitting down. Stand up."

Tooter stood up.

"Okay, now. This—" Aunt Sally swept her arm about "—is the honey house."

"I don't see any honey," said Tooter.

"That's because it ain't here," said Aunt Sally. "It's out yonder in the hives. The bees are making it. I'll be collecting it in here later this summer." She nodded to the doorway. "Let's go see the great outdoors."

Outside the honey house was a grassy hill. The near slope of the hill was fenced in. In the field a single animal grazed.

Aunt Sally pointed. "What is it?"

Tooter had seen this beast before. It was black and white and had four legs. There was a bag-like thing hanging beneath it. She was pretty sure the bag-like thing was an udder. The problem was, as far as she knew, only cows had udders.

This thing was not a cow. At least, she didn't think so.

"It's an animal," Tooter stated firmly.

"You're cookin'," said Aunt Sally. "Tell me more."

Tooter took a deep breath. "It's not...a cow."

Aunt Sally slapped her on the back. "Good girl! That there critter is not a cow and never was."

"But that *is* an udder there, isn't it?" said Tooter.

Aunt Sally nodded. "Bingo. That there is one fine upstanding all-American Grade-A udder. So tell me—" she leaned into Tooter's face "—what's that udder hanging onto?"

Tooter frowned. "This isn't school. It's summer vacation. I'm not supposed to have a test."

Aunt Sally moved in. She pressed her fingertip on the end of Tooter's nose. "This is not a test. This is punishment. And you're stalling. Answer."

Tooter squealed and stomped her foot and knew that she was out of time. She took a wild guess. "A moose?"

Aunt Sally seemed about to laugh. And then she was hugging Tooter tightly and stroking her hair. She was saying, as if to a baby or puppy, "You poor creature. Don't even know the difference between a moose and a goat. What did that awful town place do to you?"

Tooter felt like she could take a nap right there snuggled up against her aunt. Sometimes it was hard to remember that she hated this place.

"It's a goat?" she said.

"Yes, ma'am. That there is one goat."

"Goats have udders too?"

"Goats have udders too."

"Do they make milk too?"

"Like the old saying goes," said Aunt Sally. "Where there's an udder, there's milk."

A terrible thought began to wriggle into Tooter's brain. She backed away. She stared at her aunt.

"I drink milk every day."

Aunt Sally nodded. "I believe you do."

"And you're telling me the milk I drink

comes from—" she pointed at the goat "—*that?*"

Aunt Sally answered cheerily: "That's why it's called goat's milk."

Tooter's tongue shot out as if trying to escape her mouth. She gagged. She stepped backward. She felt something mushy underfoot. She looked down at her sneaker. She looked up at Aunt Sally.

Aunt Sally nodded: "Goat poop."

Tooter howled. She scrubbed her sneaker into the ground. She howled again and bolted for the house.

9

Poop

Mrs. Pepperday was waiting at the back door. "Punishment over so soon?"

"Goat milk! Goat poop!" Tooter squawked. "I'm not being punished. I'm being tortured."

Mrs. Pepperday held out a small white plastic bag. "Well, this isn't torture," she said. "This is a chore. Empty this bag in the compost heap."

Tooter took the bag. "Compost heap? What's that?"

"Ask Aunt Sally," her mother replied. She went inside.

Tooter asked Aunt Sally. Her aunt led her around the house to the vegetable garden.

She pointed to a wire fence in the shape of a circle. The fence was as tall as Tooter. Inside was a pile of dark brown oily gloppy gunky stuff.

"That's the compost heap."

Tooter pinched her nose. "Eww! It smells."

"It's supposed to smell," said Aunt Sally. "It's rotting."

"What is it?" Tooter honked through her pinched nose. "More poop?"

"That's one way of thinking of it," said Aunt Sally. "I guess you could call it plant poop. Why don't you open the bag there and dump 'er in."

Tooter opened the bag. Inside she could see the remains of breakfast. Coffee grounds, grapefruit rinds, egg shells. Her nose wrinkled.

"Garbage."

"Compost," said Aunt Sally.

"Garbage," said Tooter. "Don't you even have garbage trucks out here?"

"Sure," said Aunt Sally. "But this stuff is too good for garbage. Dump 'er in."

Tooter held the bag upside-down over the fence and let the contents fall on the heap. Then she backed off till she could no longer smell it. "That is the grossest, most disgusting thing I ever saw."

Aunt Sally grinned. "The better to grow your tomatoes with, my dear."

Tooter stared. "What are you talking about?"

Aunt Sally reached over the wire fence

and scooped up a handful of compost. Three fat worms fell out.

"Leaves, grass clippings, leftovers. That's what goes in. After half a year, this is what comes out. Best seed food in the world. This is what we plant our tomatoes in. And our lettuce and cucumbers and beans and peas and carrots and everything you see in this here garden."

Tooter looked at the garden. She was turning green. "You mean the food I've been eating grew up in that...that..."

"Like the old saying goes," chirped Aunt Sally. "Rotten earth makes sweet pea." She tossed the handful back onto the heap.

Tooter was getting woozy.

"Come on," said Aunt Sally. "We'll go see the rest of the farm."

Tooter groaned. She flopped to the ground.

"I can't take any more. I'm gonna barf."

Aunt Sally smiled gently. She thought for a moment.

"All right. Just two more things. Not punishment. You can do them by yourself whenever you feel like. Okay?"

Tooter grunted.

Aunt Sally nodded. "Okay. These are two little things you might never notice on your own. They'll show you there's more to the farm than meets the eye." She chuckled. "Or the nose."

Aunt Sally knelt down beside a group of white-topped plants. "First thing. These are called Queen Anne's lace," she said. "Someday I want you to look real close at one, and see what you find in the middle. Okay?"

Tooter grunted.

Aunt Sally walked over to a small group of trees and shrubs. "Second thing. See these plants with leaves that look like mittens?"

Tooter grunted. The leaves did look like mittens.

"They're called sassafras," said Aunt Sally. "Someday I want you to pull up one of those plants and smell the root."

"What is it?" sniffed Tooter. "A poop root?"

Aunt Sally laughed. "You'll find out."

At dinner that evening Tooter would not eat any vegetables or drink her milk. "Why does everything on a farm have to smell bad?" she grumped. "Everywhere you go, poop here, poop there. I'll bet the bees are even flying over and pooping in our hair."

Chuckie laughed.

Tooter went on talking about poop. Bee poop. Goat poop. Pig poop. Chicken poop.

Finally Mrs. Pepperday slammed down her fork.

"You've said the word poop twenty-two times," said Mr. Pepperday.

"Poop poop poop poop poop," said Tooter.

"That's twenty-seven."

"If you say that word one more time," said Mrs. Pepperday, "you may leave the table and go outside to smell the farm some more."

"Poop," said Tooter.

Chuckie cracked up.

Mrs. Pepperday pointed to the door. Tooter left the room.

"Did you turn the egg today?" Mrs. Pepperday called.

"Yes," Tooter called back, and was gone.

Ten minutes later Aunt Sally looked out the window and broke out laughing.

She waved. "Come here. You gotta see this."

Everyone went to the window. There was

Tooter, in the barnyard. She was wearing
Aunt Sally's straw hat on her head and a
clothespin on her nose. She was running
back and forth with a can of air freshener.
She was spraying the farm.

10

Countdown to Hatch

Tooter went to bed that night. But she could not sleep. She had lied to her mother. She had not turned the egg that day.

At first, she had felt fine about it. But now she kept hearing Aunt Sally's words. *If you don't do your chore, the egg will never become a chick.*

Never become...

Never become...

She could not stand it any longer. She got out of bed. She opened her door. The house was dark. And scary.

She slid her hand along the wall. She felt her way down the hall to the stairs.

She lowered herself onto one step. Then another. Halfway down the stairs, she began to see something. A faint misting of light.

She came to the bottom. She made her way through the living room. The light was still very faint. Her hands groped before her. In the dining room she could make out the tops of chairs and furniture.

And the glowing doorway to the kitchen.

There it was. One small bare bulb in the corner of the kitchen. Sixty watts of light in a world of darkness. And the egg basking like a sunbather on the beach.

On the side of the shoebox Aunt Sally had made a sign. In red crayon were the words DAYS TILL HATCH. Then came a piece of paper with a number. The number was 14.

Tooter screeched: "Fourteen days to go!"

She clamped her mouth shut. Had she woken someone up?

She glared at the egg.

She whispered, "Are you crazy? I'm not turning you for fourteen more days. What do I look like? Your mother?"

She jabbed her finger at the egg. "Three more days...okay, four...o-*kay*, five. That's it. Counting today. If you ain't out in five days—" she pressed the egg with her fingertip "—you can turn yourself."

She gave the egg a quarter-turn. She started to leave, and discovered she did not want to go. It was warm and bright where the light bulb was. Safe and friendly. She wished she was small enough to crawl into the shoebox with the egg.

But she wasn't.

Tooter looked at the kitchen window, at the blackness beyond. She looked at the back

door. Was it locked? Was someone, some *thing* even now reaching for the doorknob, about to look in the window?

She got out of there—fast. She groped and bumped and stumbled her way back through the dining room and living room and up the stairway and down the hallway to her room. She plunged into her bed and cuddled and curled till her nose met her knees and pulled the sheet over herself like a shell and shivered herself to sleep.

11

Better Be Careful

Several days later Tooter was outside teaching Chuckie how to spit long-distance.

"Tooter!" called Mrs. Pepperday.

Her mother was waiting in the kitchen. She had a scowl on her face.

She pointed to the shoebox. "Is this your doing?"

"Is what?" said Tooter.

"You know what," said her mother. "Don't act innocent."

Tooter walked over to the shoebox. The sign now said 11 days till hatching. She

65

looked in. There was the egg, dozing on its side.

But there was a second egg too. Standing in the corner. With a face. A terrible face drawn in crayon. A face with a wicked mouth and green, daggery teeth. A face with purple skin and horns. A face with eyes yellow and evil. Eyes that glared at the other egg.

"What is it?" said Tooter. "Some kind of voodoo egg?"

"Funny you should say that," said her mother. "I was thinking the same thing. It looks like someone is trying to cast a spell on the good egg."

Tooter stared at her mother. "Who would do that?"

Her mother squeezed Tooter's cheeks until her mouth was like a fish's. "You would do that, little miss, because you don't like it here. So you're trying sabotage."

"What's sabotage?" said Tooter through her fish mouth. She hated having her cheeks squeezed.

"Sabotage," said her mother, "is messing things up so you can get your own way. Like sneaking into your father's computer and sticking yourself into his story. Like putting a pair of my earrings on Harvey's ears."

Tooter looked shocked. "You think I did all that?"

Her mother snorted. "No, I think the tooth fairy did it." She let go of her daughter's cheeks. She took the voodoo egg from the box and gave it to Tooter. "Throw this on the compost heap."

Tooter screeched, "I hate the compost heap!"

Her mother pointed to the door.

"Do I have to do it if I confess?" said Tooter.

"Yes."

Tooter stomped her foot, stuck her tongue out at the good egg, and left.

Tooter hated it when her mother had everything figured out. What was the point of confessing? She was glad she didn't.

And now she had a name for her recent activities: sabotage. That was interesting.

Tooter headed for the compost heap. She had a great idea. She didn't have to get near enough to smell it. All she had to do was pitch the egg from a safe distance. Which she did.

The egg fell short.

Tooter pinched her nose, stomped up to the wire fence and threw the egg over. At least it was hard-boiled.

Walking away, Tooter spotted the white-topped weeds. The ones Aunt Sally had called Queen Anne's lace.

Look real close at one, and see what you find in the middle.

Tooter picked one out. She looked. It was lacy, all right. Like a doily. Round. The size of a small pancake.

She knelt down to look closer. There was a faint odor of carrots. Yes, there *was* something in the middle of the lace. A spot. A fleck. So small you'd never notice unless you got this close.

The spot was black—no, purple. She looked closer, squinting, straining her eyeballs.

It was a flower.

The teeniest, tiniest flower she had ever seen. It would take a whole bouquet of them to cover her fingernail. An almost-invisible purple flower keeping its secret in a white, carroty bed of lace.

"Wow."

What else had Aunt Sally said?

Pull up one of those plants and smell the root.

Mitten-shaped leaves. Sassafras. She found one. She pulled it from the earth. The root didn't look different from any other root. She smelled it. She took off running.

She found Aunt Sally in the barn.

She wagged the root under her nose. "Root beer!"

Aunt Sally smiled. "Root beer it is. And did you find anything in the Queen Anne's lace?"

"Sure did," said Tooter. "A purple flower. The world's littlest."

Aunt Sally shook her finger at Tooter. "Better be careful, or you might become a farmer."

"No way," said Tooter, laughing.

At dinner Mr. Pepperday said, "You

know, that egg in there has been in the family for a while now. Don't you think we ought to give it a name?"

"Humpty Dumpty!" blurted Chuckie.

"Arf!" said Harvey.

"Bubblebutt," said Tooter.

"Eggbert," said Mr. Pepperday.

The three grownups agreed. Eggbert it was.

"Now, remember everybody," said Aunt Sally. "When the time comes, no giving Eggbert a helping hand. Chicks have to fight their way out of the shell. That's how they get the gumption to take on the world."

Aunt Sally poured herself a glass of milk.

"And another thing," she said. She took a long swallow from her glass. "The first critter it sees when it comes out of that shell, that's who it's gonna call Mama."

Chuckie laughed. "Maybe it'll be Harvey!"

Harvey arfed.

Tooter said nothing. It was not until after dinner that she realized she had eaten her vegetables.

12

Two Tooters

Nine days till hatching...

Eight days...

Seven days...

Day after day Tooter heard: "Did you turn Eggbert? Did you turn Eggbert?" It was worse than "Did you brush your teeth?"

She wished everybody would stop nagging her. Maybe then she could figure out if she liked the darn thing or not.

Sometimes it seemed there were two Tooters now. One Tooter, the old one, hated having only two TV channels. The new

Tooter went out each day to look at the tiny purple flowers.

The old Tooter held her nose and went "Eww!" every time she passed the barn. The new Tooter breathed deeply and went "Ahh!" as she boiled sassafras roots with Aunt Sally.

The old Tooter would not go near goat's milk. The new Tooter drank chocolate goat's milk for breakfast.

The old Tooter listened each evening for the ring of the Jack and Jill truck. The new Tooter heard the song of a meadowlark.

The old Tooter turned off Eggbert's light. The new Tooter turned it right back on.

Three days…

Two days…

And then the old Tooter went away and never came back. It happened with one day left till hatching. And it happened in the barnyard.

Besides turning Eggbert, Tooter had another chore that day. She had to feed the chickens. Aunt Sally had given her a can of seeds and cracked corn.

In the barnyard she walked about casting feed onto the ground. Five chickens and the

rooster came cackling and pecking.

One of the chickens was busily pecking away when another chicken charged and sent it squawking. There was a flurry of brown feathers. The bully chicken started pecking in the other's place.

Tooter recognized the bully. It was Drumsticks, the hen that laid Eggbert.

Now it was Tooter who came charging.
"Who do you think you are? You're not just
dumb—you're mean!"

Drumsticks squawked and fled.

Tooter went after her. "You ought to be
ashamed of yourself! There's an egg in that
house and it's supposed to be yours and you
don't even care! What kind of a mother are
you?"

Tooter chased the chicken in circles till
she got dizzy and gave up. Drumsticks went
back to pecking as if nothing had happened.
As if feeding her own gizzard was all that
mattered in the world.

Tooter knew that her own mother would
never be so heartless.

And Tooter knew what she had to do.

13

The Longest Night

Before going to sleep that night, Tooter set her Yogi Bear alarm clock on Spring. That meant twelve o'clock midnight.

When the alarm went off, she couldn't believe she had been asleep for three hours. It felt like three minutes.

She dragged herself out of bed. This time she had a flashlight waiting. She followed the beam of light down the dark hallway, down the stairs, through the living room and dining room to the kitchen.

She looked into the shoebox and let out a

squeal of joy. It had already begun. The shell
on one end was cracked.

Tooter squealed again as the shell wob-
bled slightly. The crack grew a bit. She

thought she saw the end of a tiny beak.

Tooter lay down on her stomach. She propped her chin in her hands and smiled and watched. Every minute or so she giggled.

It amazed her to think that inside that smooth, brown shell, an egg had become Eggbert.

Tooter remembered Aunt Sally's words. *No giving Eggbert a helping hand.*

But Aunt Sally did not say you couldn't root for it.

Tooter made a fist.

"Come on," she whispered. "You can do it."

The crack grew slowly. Tooter's sleepy eyes kept closing and snapping open. The crack became a circle. The shell now had a lid.

Tooter could see the lid move. She knew Eggbert was inside poking with all his might.

"Come on...you can do it."

Tooter drifted in and out of sleep. She kept seeing herself and Eggbert. They were alike, weren't they? The two of them? Both taken from their cozy nests and dumped in a strange place. She on a farm, he in a shoebox.

Tooter and Eggbert...

Eggbert and Tooter...

And then her eyes were open again. There he was, poking through a hole in the lid. Half a scrawny face, beak and eye, looking straight up at her.

Somewhere outside the rooster crowed. Night withdrew from the windowpane.

Tooter felt the warmth of the light bulb on her face and in her heart. She smiled weakly. She greeted the newborn chick. "Hi, Eggbert."

She closed her eyes.

The rest of the family came down for breakfast. They heard the peeping, then saw the fluffy yellow chick. Tooter was curled around the shoebox, fast asleep.

Mrs. Pepperday knelt down and smiled at her daughter. "Miss Tooter, you never cease to amaze me."

"Looks like Mama and baby are doing fine," said Aunt Sally.

Chuckie and Harvey sat quietly by the box, looking in.

Mr. Pepperday chuckled. "I think Tooter Pepperday has finally joined the rest of us hogs in the slop."

Don't miss the next Tooter Pepperday book!

How will Tooter Pepperday cope with her responsibilities as the mama of a newborn chick?

Will she ever lead a normal life without pizza and McDonald's?

Will she overcome her horror and disgust of the dreaded compost heap?

Find out when you read about Tooter Pepperday's next encounters with farmyard critters in another hilarious book by Jerry Spinelli.

About the Author

None of Jerry Spinelli's six children was ever saddled with the responsibility of baby-sitting an egg, but his daughter Molly was just as persistent with him as Tooter Pepperday is with her father. While writing one of his books, Jerry didn't hear his daughter calling him until she sat on his desk and began writing him a note vertically along the page of his longhand manuscript! He told her to "Scoot!" but paid more attention to her next time she came into the room.

Other books by Jerry Spinelli include *Fourth Grade Rats, The Bathwater Gang,* and *Maniac Magee,* for which he won the Newbery Medal in 1991. Jerry lives with his wife, Eileen, also a children's book author, in Phoenixville, Pennsylvania.

	DATE DUE		